as
k
vision

Printed in the United States of America

First Printing, Hardback, 2020
Paperback 2023

Hardback ISBN: 978-1-7347545-2-0
Paperback ISBN: 978-1-955498-02-9

Press Here
410 S Michigan Ave Suite 420
Chicago, IL 60605

www.mattbodett.com

a

novel

what it was
was

    carrying a burden

    like fighting rain

part

on e

(construct

vision)

clearly sound not way to

form can simply

and cause the way
It is cast to

be the found
the way to be
founding

These days seem to

one or
another

quite easily
clean
the safe windows

and i picked the
four sounds that

seemed to play

in the ear of

company

and the sound of the

Company

to cheer the

wind of rain

~~the~~ it seems sound

the day to make sound
in pain   or   to
be casting stones in
rain
water to
sail like the

it was
it could be
a boat for sailing

or a stone for
casting the

one

remember

and the company of
sound in ear of rain

In the could of

sailing without
wind
is fresh to   be

with the

way

friends

take days

to

smile

to remember the
hand is in the
wind

forward is toward

singing the stubborn

hunts

and when mine

when head
of
the way they
seem to linger on
their names for
~~class~~

they name
the sounded of
me to sings the
way fewer than
not cast like some
cast the fingers toward
It was hurt
and when asked it
was more
than
when they made
roads to
smooth

to   seem   there

        is   me   in   sounds

        of   names

in   common   ing   it

        was   more   than

canceling

        it   was   more

like   flowing   into

names   of   boats

        to
sail

the way to sounde

the common toss

session of hearing
mine ~~of~~ or this
was the

rock sound

on
water sound

and sinking

toward more names of

sings with not rhymes

with

and future finding or

fresh burns and there

wasn't any way that

the smoke could rise

further

than the covers

there wasn't any
way that the toward
was cast
in the same
hand of
really care or of

really know
and ~~they~~ they seem
to feel that
~~forget~~ is the
feeling

or the name for the

casting rocks into

Sounds

of names in the

same manner that

one can feel the

same toward

the total cast

the

toll

cast ing

the ing   the final

is   a   way

it   was   a   name   that

the final   was   to
                   ward

was   to

ward   off   the

stranger &   fear   is   the
            same

like the e   names

they gave

and m casting names
  toward

it was the way it
  tastet

     well   not

single is not the same
    as afraid
    or singing like rain
                  sailing

    for

the words came to

seem that

being was the not

single boat of found

what happens when

you can't say
names

too many skies

too many finding

shapes in rain puddles
that

too many

stones

flat sound rust

not

to

to

ward no

really   feeding   the
way   of   fleeted

of   flee

what   does   it   mean
to   say

to   run

like   a   mouth

or   wild ?

total sounds of
care and when they
think it
was not all the
same as
saying sorry as
the same as feeling
the cast

it was in the name
of what giving

and it
was given to
make the sense sound
in the
way that names
made order
or
made
it order

and the whash of single

namet

water

sound

what happens to the final
wishet name to
the way that
hands hurt
to touch when
its all the way
of burdens to
keep
sounds

wishing to knee to
find the sample
of
single
same

as the w

breathe

was not toward
too many
SKIES

but still the way to
say that there were
more cases in

the way
to find
the borders at the

names like the

way
of sinking

stones

how it can simply

seem

then to see that

when we never

find

hands in the

way pockets hold

to sound

to re

member

It is in the
        asking

not   in   the way
    words are   sound

    you   seem to

        find nothing
        can be easy to
            know when to
            read the language
        of stone
            Sounds

turning into the

sounds of when

the sky was

also the

way that when

grass leaves

a stain

and it

tastes like the

bitter

forms

the

bitter

cast   eyes   that

want   to   know   if   It   is

hard   to

when   it   is   hard   to

sound   and   it

must   make   things

So

hard

they are there to
sound the notes of
each page
of running the
just way to
be sometimes
withe
something to
say I am
going to

ward ffhe way to
gather

the grass on jeans
of sound

for too long there

wa saying that
it wa
only good

to act like walking
didnt mean
falling

but there

was   a   way   to   hold
the   curtain
and   the
safe
and   the
way to   hold the

beginning   of   being

in   holding

to   be   talking
toward   sounds   of

please

when we know that
hands seem to
cast the same waves
Sailing

boats

and where
Sing

and it is
hold

there was near to
be hold rise
the same as flags
on the

same skies toward
the bothered
rain
there rain holds
the seldom
wind
In the two hands
toward the
names of boats

when the same
sound again

and the same names
hurting there

is no

holding hand to
simply cast with

pockets of stones
and beaches

when there was
just simply

the glasses of taking
fresh

rain sounds out of the
way of days

worth of examining
burdens to

be

precisely the same as
samples of pockets of
boats

It is a name that
sounds

like
problem

finding a site of an old

way of crashing

against the same

sound of

liking the

same way to

contact feeling

like clothes
too many times
worn

except for the same
names of rainy skies

which are burdens
on slippery stairs

it is another way to
examine
the same
names

it was never about refunds

It was always about
            pockets

and the   keeping

    why did it seem
        safe when it

    war
        stones

there is always the
name of rain

and the
sounding of
rains of
being slippery

and of walking
in the same
direction you
are speaking

although i forget what the
name for that

is

like being a passing
sound to
something

breathing

it was about some kind of
pain
that was for hearing

and their names

for sounding good names
clearly

hit the surface of
the raining

and it was
always about the way
the boat sank

or the way it still
sank on top of
the rain
Sounds

like careful reading
toward a way to
know there
really doesn't have
to be a method
for smiling as ~~s~~ for
casting a shadow

or for trying to be
perfect about crying
like the rain

for only knowing that
it was their
method

walking and with both
feet moving
and maybe it was
the way toward the
sound of the same
voice but

maybe it was
also toward the
safe window or the
curtain

for drawing

and then for

casting it toward the

burden and

the name of burden

which sound

familiar and sound

is chasing the dodge

the move and

when the boat

sank

why did it still have
a name

you know what to call

the pain of

seeing the same

sound the
seeing the same
fist
and loosely cast

and why did they

want me alone

i could still practice

tying the skies
together

and finding a way
to trace the
stones into the

similar shapes
of maybe not
smiles

but really there is
something familiar
to
see in the way
that the
rain hits the
same sinking
and the same
stone
smile

forming   sounded

and

rained   and

pleased

with   no

way   to   regret

the   casual   sinking

or   sounded

in   raining

with pleased eyes
and
with simple ways
of
returning
too many crashes
of sounds like
stones in pockets
of safe
harbors and
single names

they call them
Kindness

new names for
getting

new names

for

casting aside

forget

for the movement
to get
the sound
it must
fall

yours is a simple
walk

Something something
stones

as   casual   burdens
    and broken.

        flesh

we all turn back around
    to   names

can   it be more like a
        question

because when it seems
like a burn
like when it burns
to seem
hot but really
its just

noticing that you
cant forget

Its casual rain and
still smiles

and suddenly there are so
many ways to spell
crash

to spell the wrong title
                or the same
                song

                or the way to
                drag sound across
                the dry mud

    its   a burnet
            name

        surface

        and hand
        with a
        name to
        cross

to simple too cross the
fever of cures

to name the dragging
of teeth across the
mud

too many

single fights

not enough wars

too count the
days of longing
to find nothing in
the pockets

to crash again into
the same boat that
already sank and to
sing the chorus of the
same wind and the
carols of the title skies
without knowing any
of the words to
fight them from stinging
in the belly of
fresh water falling
into drops from
rain and
stinging
stones
for

really finding the fast
wish the swiftest
curse
to

find the
singest

flattery to boast

the word
of weight
from sinking

if it was   really

about   eyes

it wouldnt

stain

its more   about

cost

like burdens that
light and

foreign songs
too many boat
burdens
for the
seas
to
hide them
all

too many ways to
sink

for many naming
to way too

smile the same

cast and call the

single most sound

in the

pocket

of rain and really

wash the careful

wind noise wish wish

when does there seem
to call the
ways of cashing out
the ways to seem the
wind of
it was too many days
of the wanted to.
when was there a
day of rest and
why did i
take it

too many names to
sink in them
all

too washing   too feeling

too smiling
    smiling
    too crasht

    too burdent

when to call the
    same tokens of
    calling the same
    ways to feel
    the same way of
    too many sounding

and then it was the
way to be done and
there was a shaking
sound of a

rattle sound of

a was there

too many ways

~~to~~ name the
ways that
there is a pain
in the back of
the way of
thinking

a way to chew the

soft part of
the smile

to pass
the time it only took
one hour to pass the
way to see the
other name that was
catching up to
smging the sounds of
falling like walking
but with fear
and no
hand

if it was a burden
too many ways
to spell take this

more likely
to
shuffle the
past into
stones and
cast into pockets

clean the safe windows

raining

it is flushed

in cheek

numb in tounque
and finger nail

side ways to sound out
the last way to
stand

to crash is standing
on the dry mud

to really see there
is nothing
focus

on the rinsed sound
   in the rain sounds hard
                      er
        than the stone
            sounds quick
                       er
                than th
                     e
                washin
                     g

it was the soft eyes

or the ~~quiet~~
              silent
         humm

it was in the noise of
   caring to hear

too soft to carry the
         hearing

mine is there really
      quick name

to really

   sound
   bitter

like pills to say
         swallow

part

two

(for the
dancers))

swings

f o l l l

o mm s

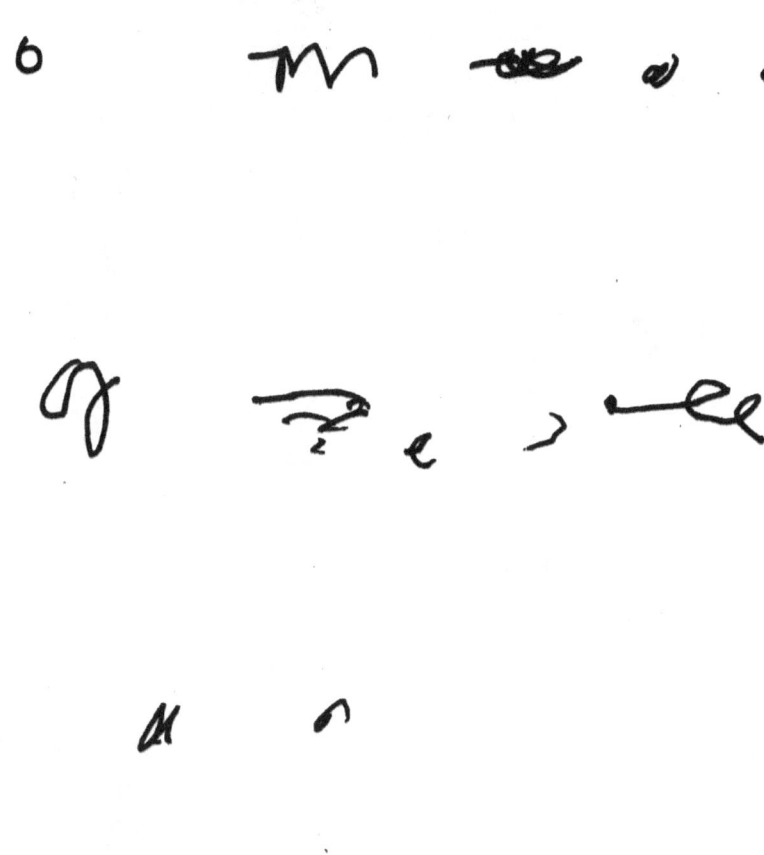

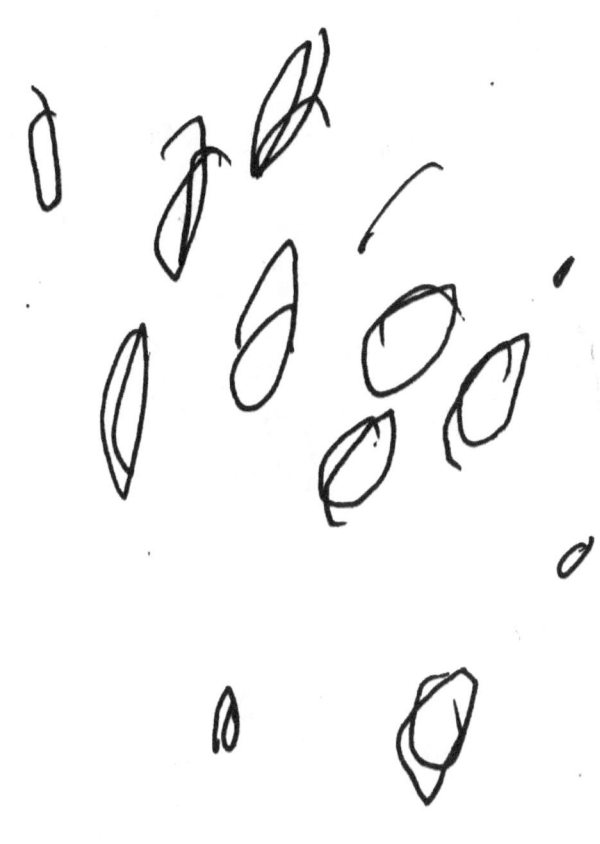

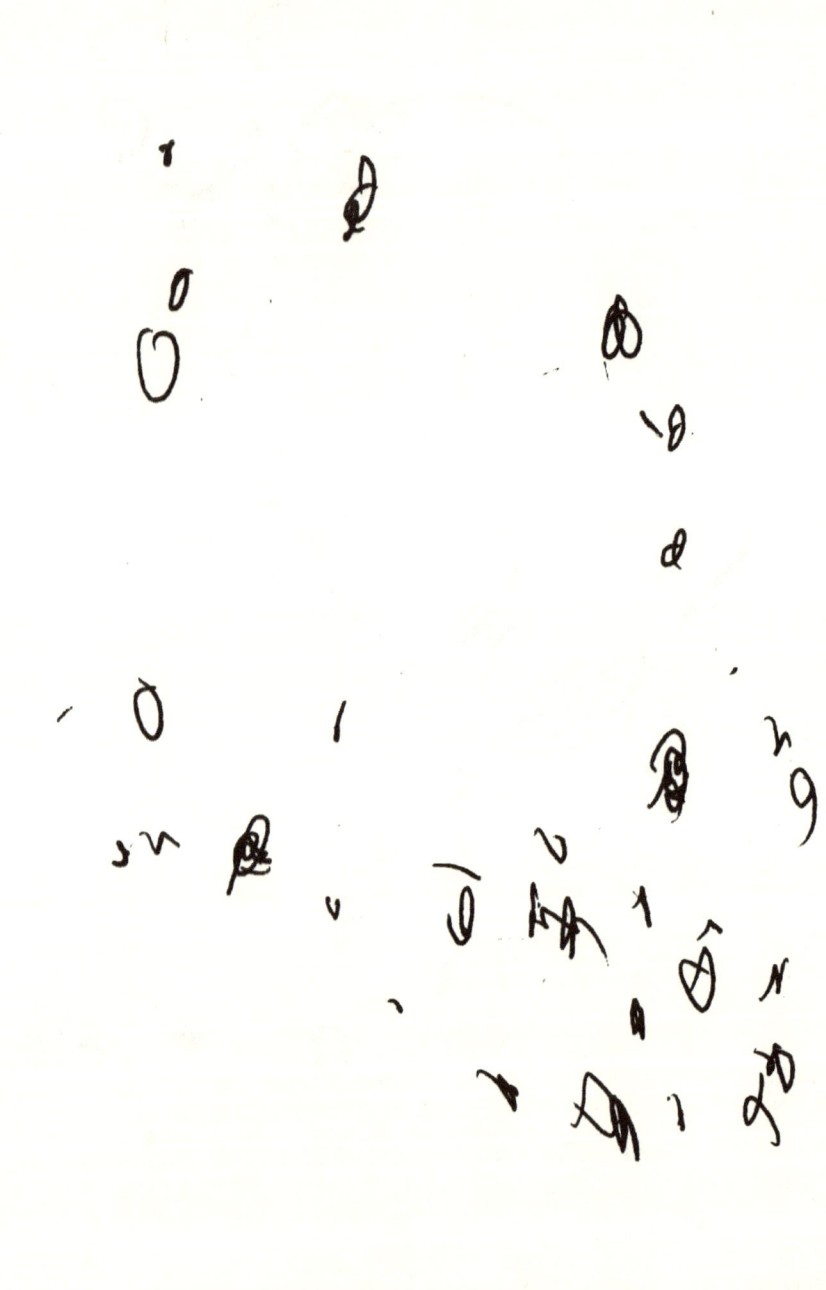

burden

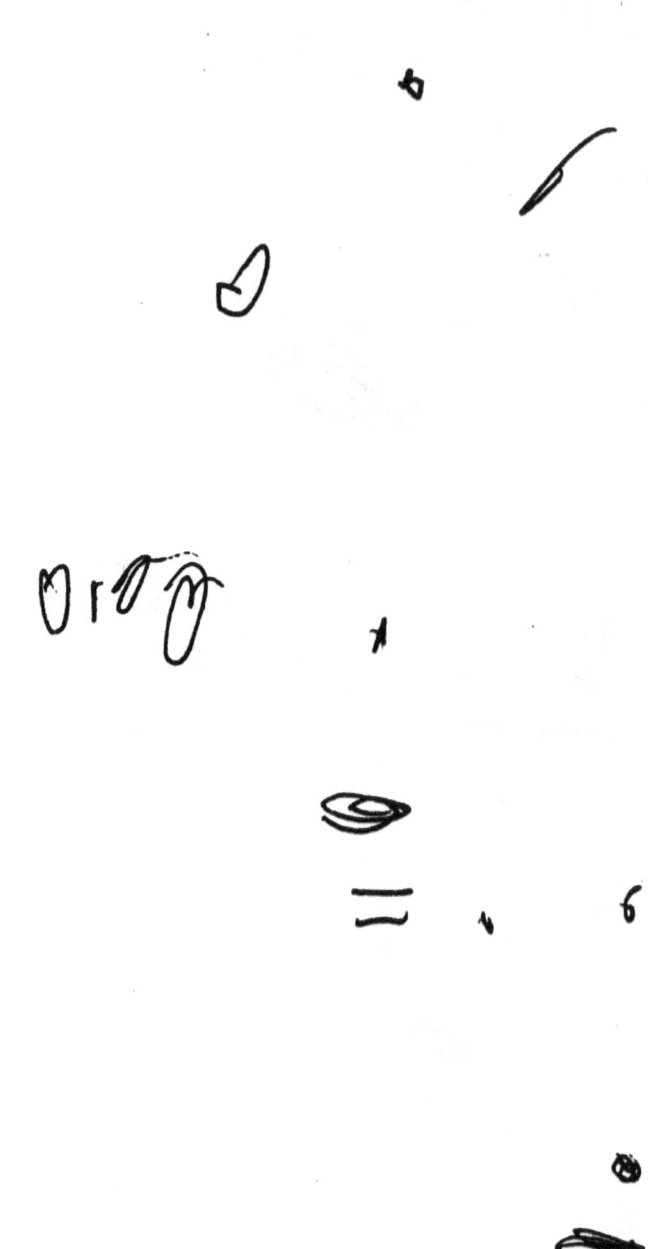

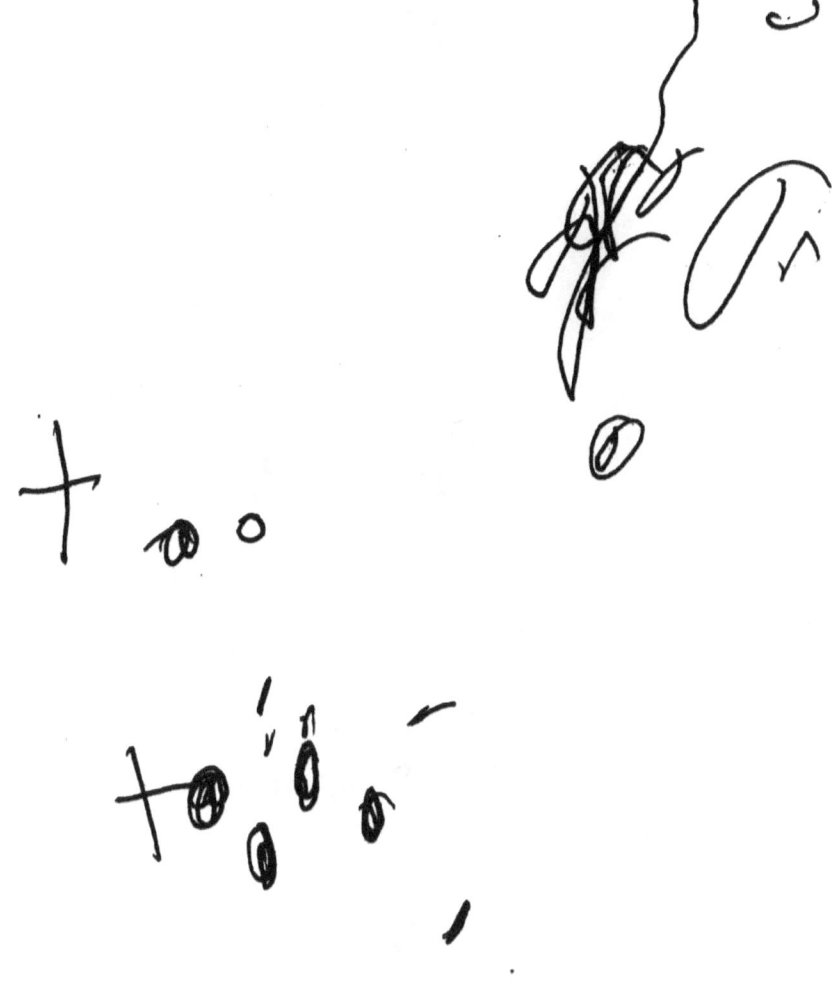

h ° ° ° ° ° ° ° ° ° ° ° ° ° ° ° ° ° °

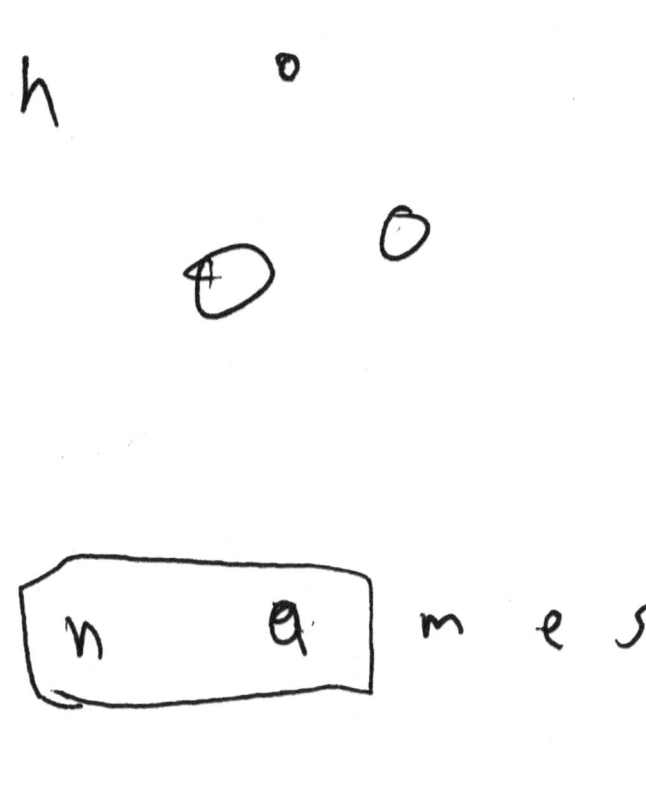

h o o

n a m e s

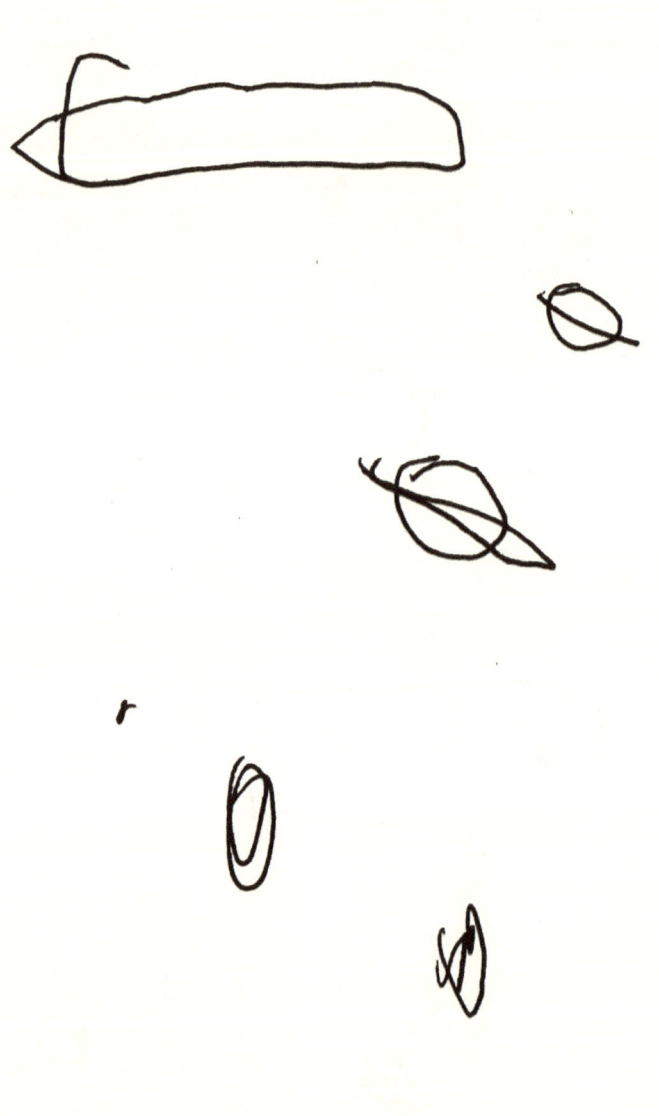

100

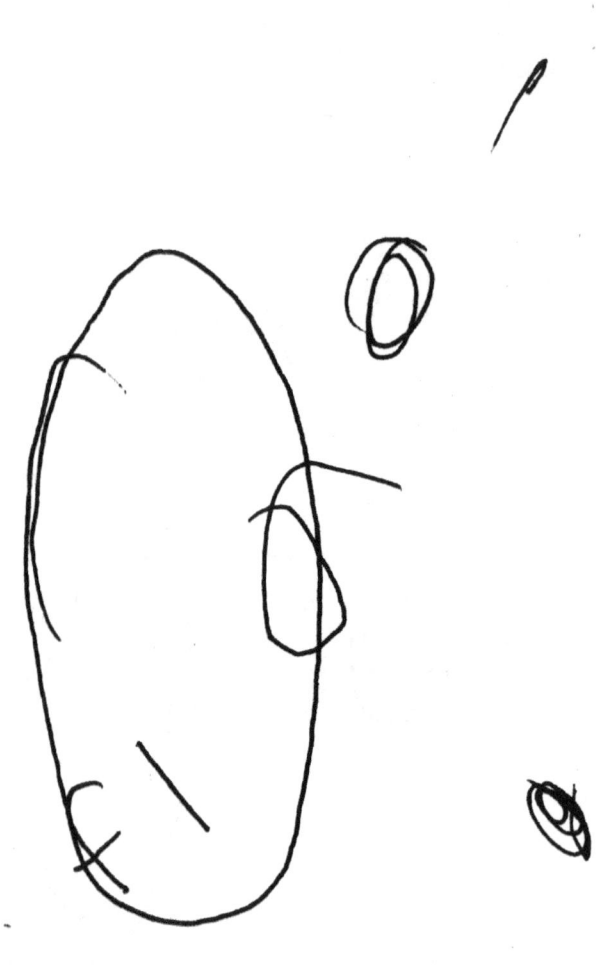

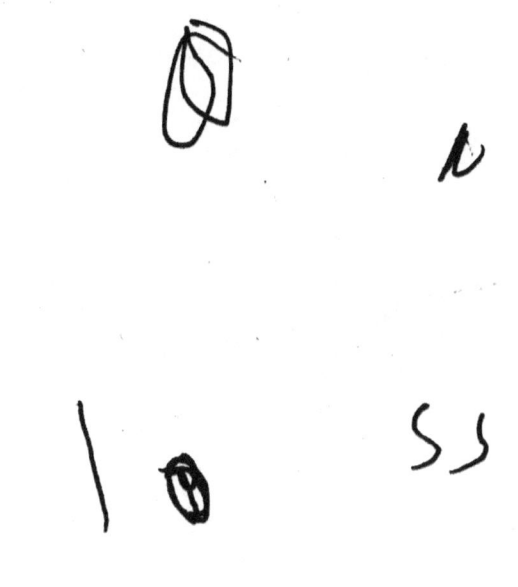

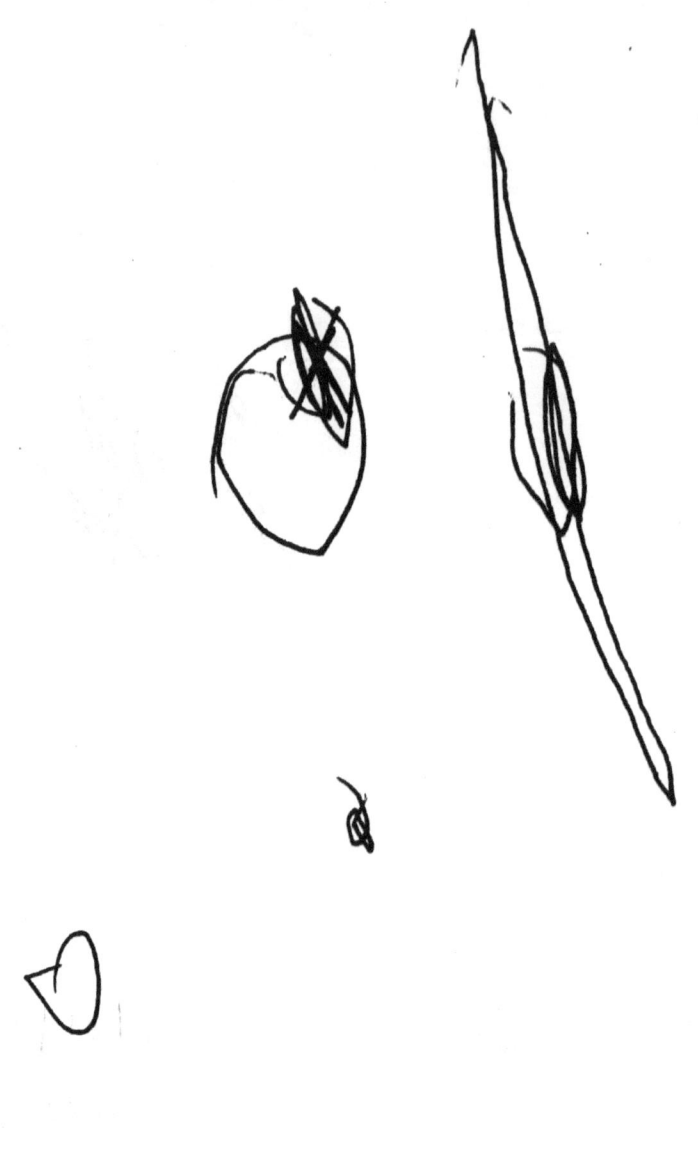

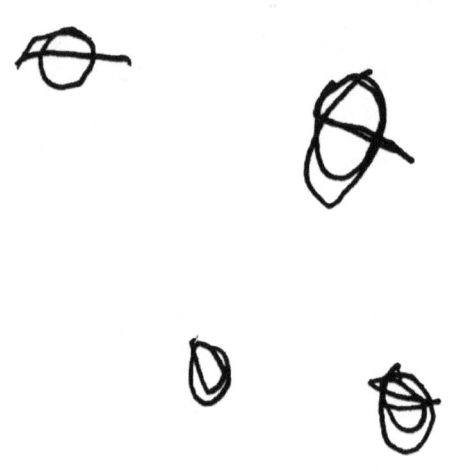

O   D

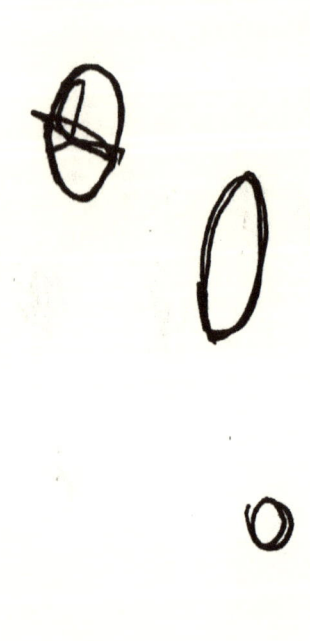

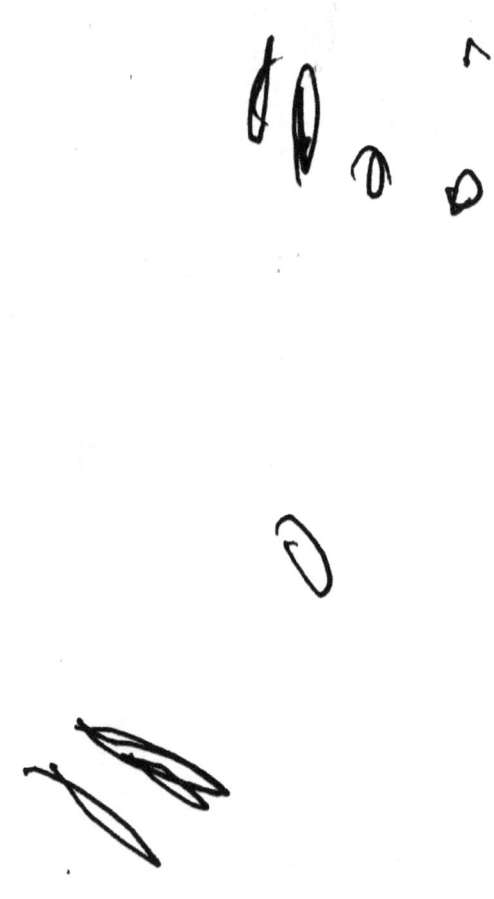

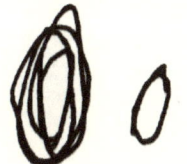

part
three

(where they find
a hals painting
in
the
attic)

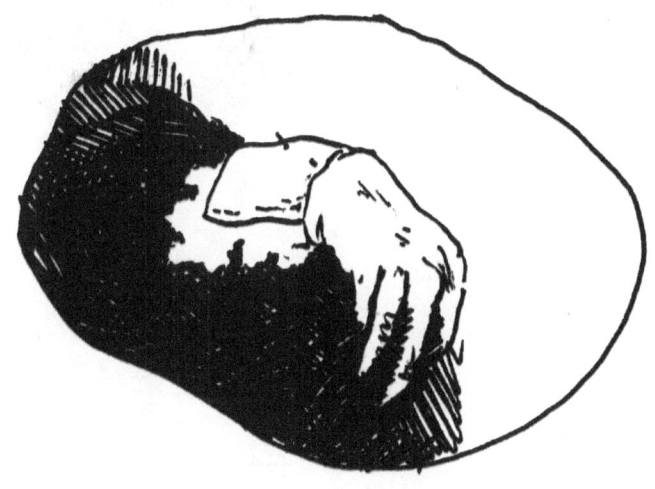

part

four

(strike the
poet)

pleaset to pass the

stain
cathedral

with the
safe window

view of sun and
there
words to

lose the single noise
of trouble

who can't wait to
pass the
saying

for place to mean that
there is
something to
lose
and a hat for
keeping the
soft
warm

where the singing is
pulling the look
of
washing the
dirt off of a
hero
and finding
bruises

to prove that it
   seems there
also lost the same

   place of mind the
   way it is more in
the trying to sing

   the candle
   burns

and it melts on the
   wood floor

it really seems to
lay the same
notions of sinking

or the same
way to think of
notions of letting go

to see the
name pass under
neath

the water level

it was like
a warning
to lay a
weary head
on the
soft

and the damage was
dragging teeth
and then the way
that bones sound dry
when they aren't
bleeding

or I can see sometimes
the
precious way it can
leave a
stain
to hold a hand
over the candle
burns

that mess with the
water to make it
                flowing there
        is
        not a
            way to
            change
                the
                    seeming
            creature th
                        at

                sings

about the water as
        it boils the
            breaking
        sense of
        kindness

for there feels to
    seem oh to know
      that true holds
not on feet
    but turns on
            the casting like
                    shadow
        with the
        young way to
            forget

words   are   spoken

and   decay
    feels   like

air swinging hard
to remember
the way to
tell
a secret
like a joke
like a stair
case

like a dry
mud

boat with no more
reasons to sink
in shallow
breathing

and dragging to say
that there is truth
in the
fire that
consumes
what
stones falter
and where
name can cause
bruises
like pain
or like favors

to swing the way to
come home
to the
faster brick
to throw
into
safe
window and
hear that the
cathedral word is
really a way of
fighting and
young and
mind

solving the safety
of right

with speaking
to know sound

we can stay

to really keep shine
to right
thats the sound of

knowing speaking

and to really hear
sorry

feel

but for now   we   cast

at   the   new   wood

floor   and

watch

rain   to   soft

touches   spell

out   sounds

of   catching

fist   fulls

and   chewing

the   soft

acre

with foundation of
hear
the looking of
breath

and have a single
problem know to

change the
when to   ask for

ashes to poke
into crying
Sounds and
sweet

pains

it wasnt   hear

but   seem

and   there   were

fourteen   masks

in the window   and

I   couldnt   see

through   any

of

them

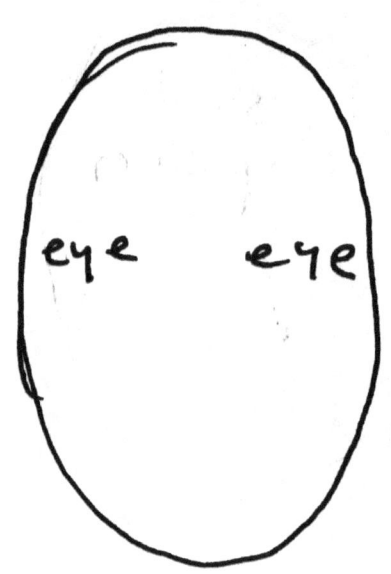

rhymes
with

delicious

so meth
ing
complic
at
ed

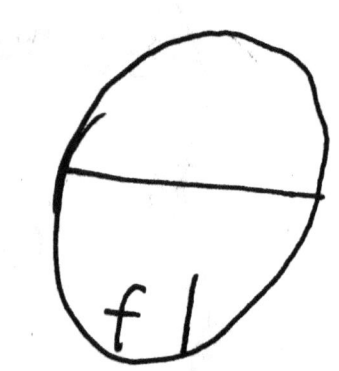

like
your
na
me

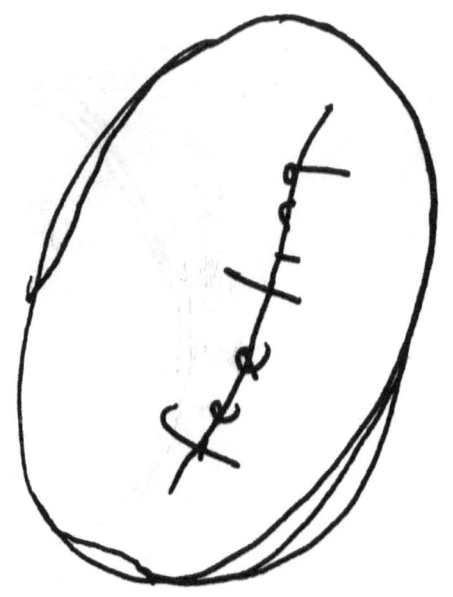

too
far
from
stars

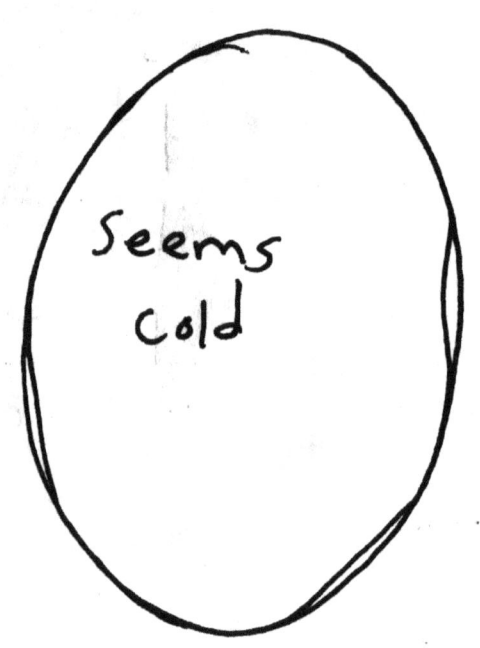

Somehow it is like slipping
   to carry on

or softly closing the
faded way to close eyes
and losing the
never way
to skin the knee in rain
   and sting the
   burning empty
   window
   stain

it's light to see the
bone the
singing boat
sinking rain
to seem like
farther casting
to ride
as a passanger
that kills
talking
for the same
way to run
into the shade
of hiding

and we are really
 playing the far
way to be cold in the
            soft

      we might be
    slowly placed beside
        the burden like
            dust
        and in the blood
    way to be far fromm
    passt

    paining

is that wind
or stopping
or a play to tell
something about

breaking

with sounded
singing
for the year
to see them
become
Circles
like the way
to practice smiling

between scale and
         fear to being
         the same shape
         of wind that
stained of raining water
     on false names
     on worn boats
   with same sounds of
         fearing the
     way wind
     really sinks in the
              ear

part
five

(or
other
ways
to
fall)

Simple

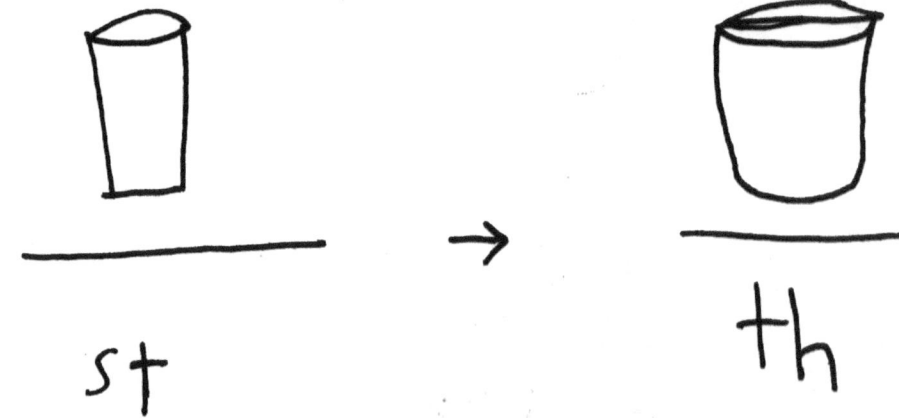

$$\frac{}{st} \rightarrow \frac{}{th}$$

place

~~place~~

~~Slow~~

$$\frac{same}{custom} =$$

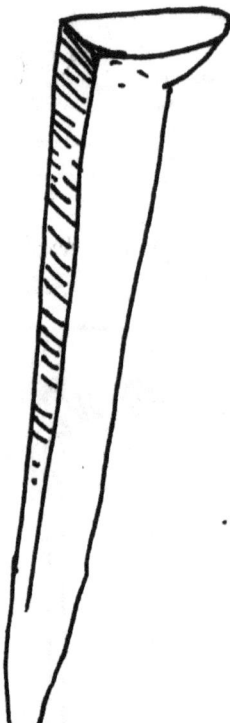

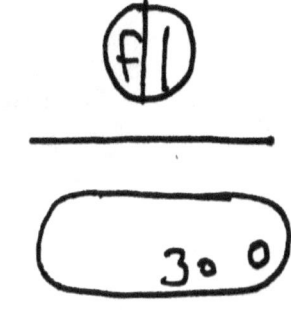

echo

―――――――――――
swall
ow

#

―――――――――――
place

$$\frac{ft}{\frac{st}{\frac{ht}{\frac{ct}{\frac{tt}{lt}}}}}$$

tt
t

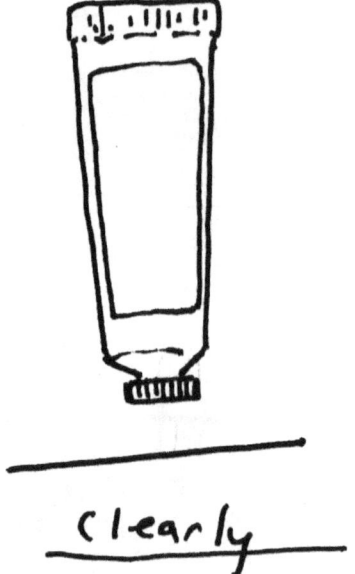

clearly

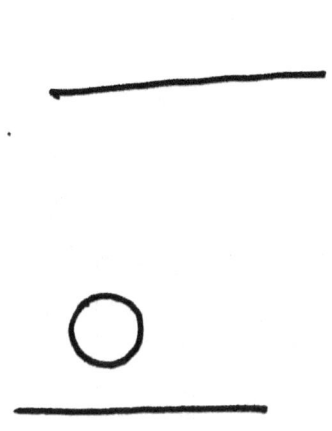

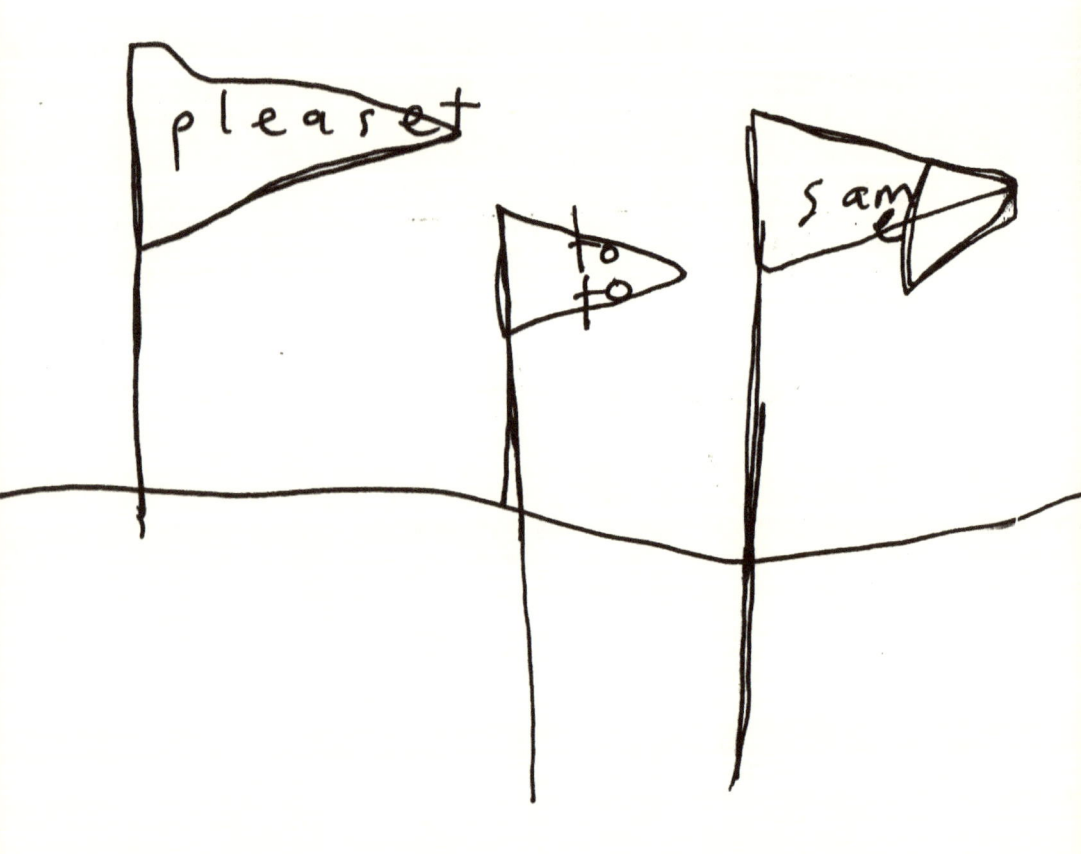

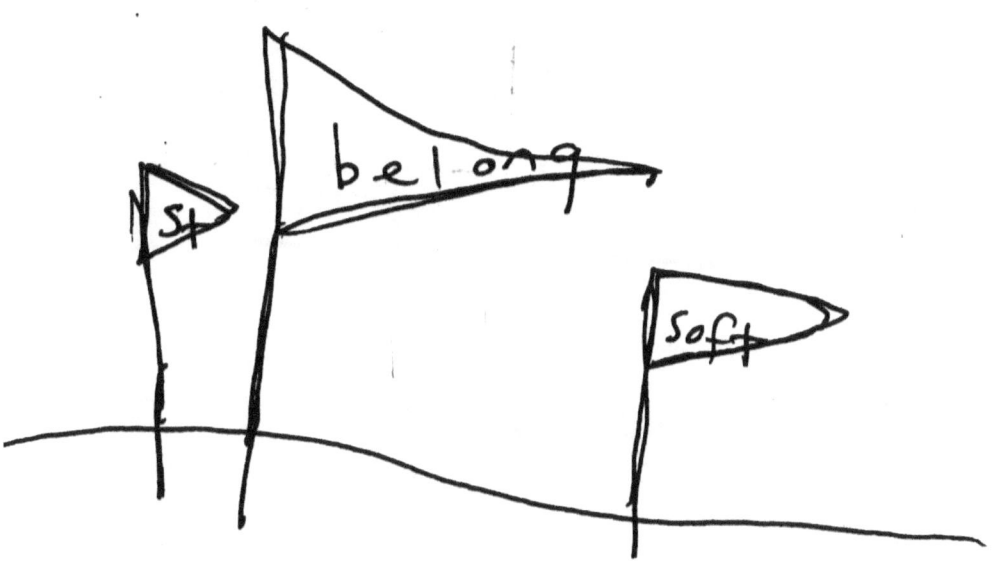

sound

fog

walk

beau ty

~~take~~

~~take~~

to

long

pain
ting

$$\frac{fear}{\frac{your}{named}}$$

proposed

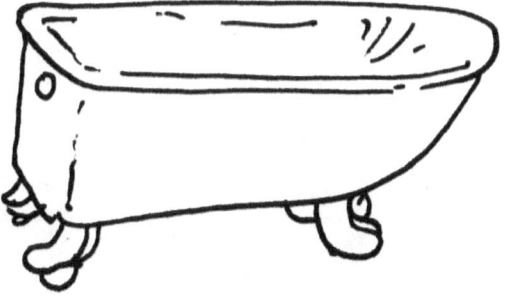

when
it
rains it
is
Sometimes
like
hearing

fell
ow

ston e

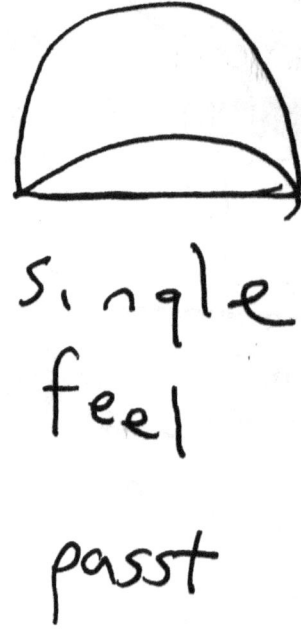

single
feel

passt

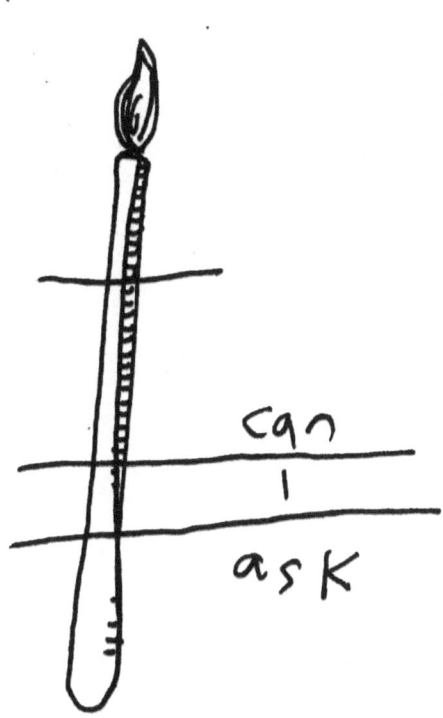

can
|
ask

$$\overline{ash}$$

can
it
seem
   like

sail

part six

(the scenery)

is

silent

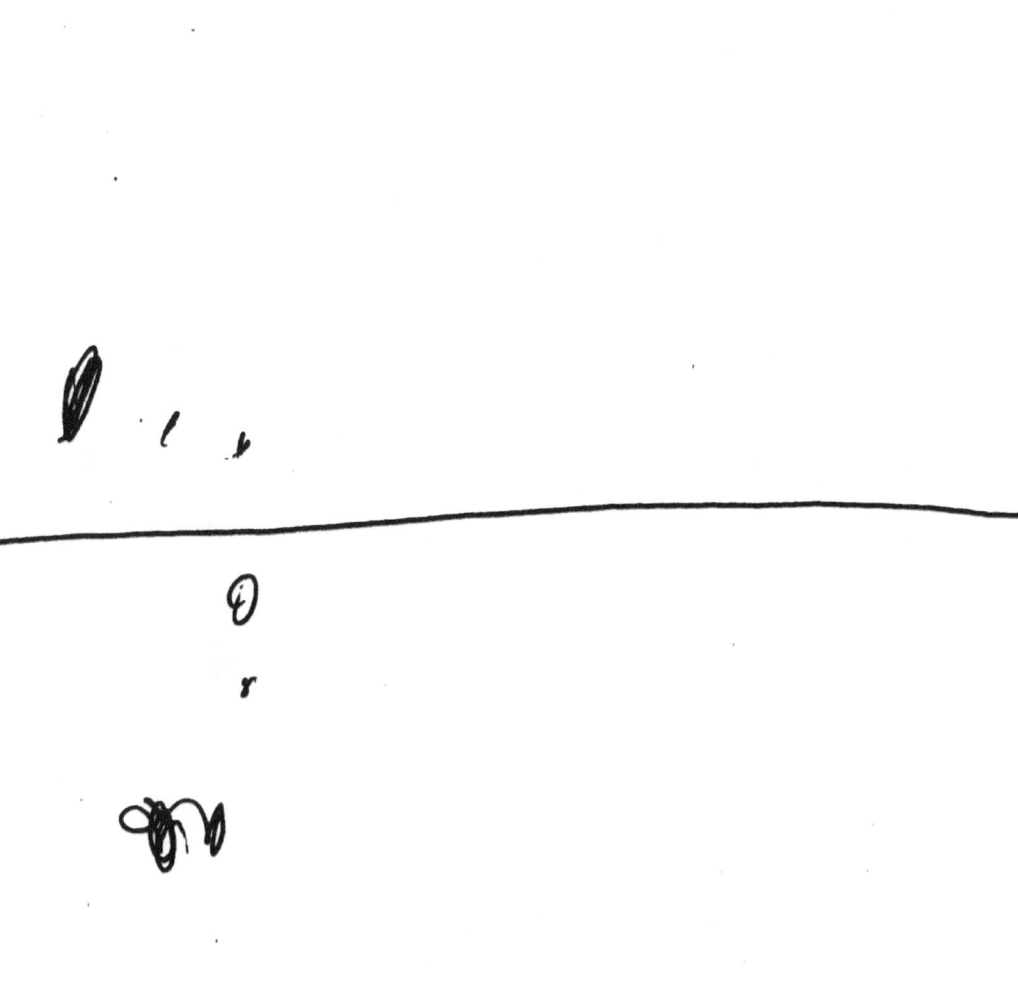

o ᵗᴴ Oₑₙ

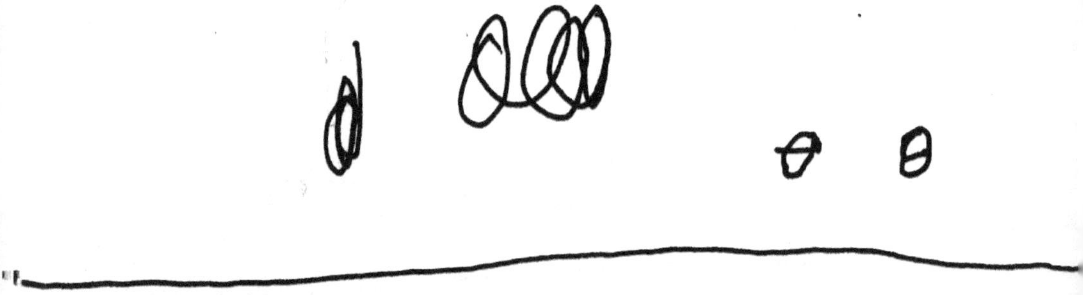

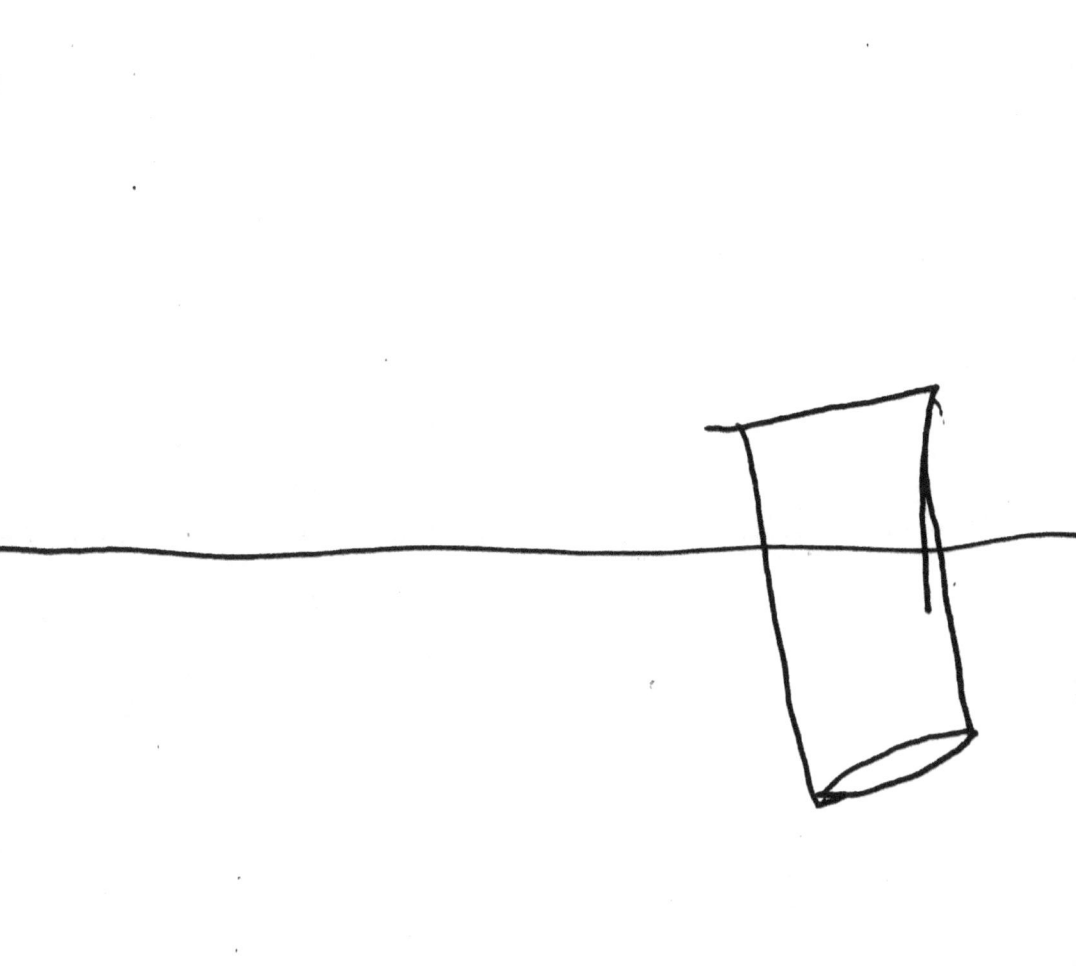

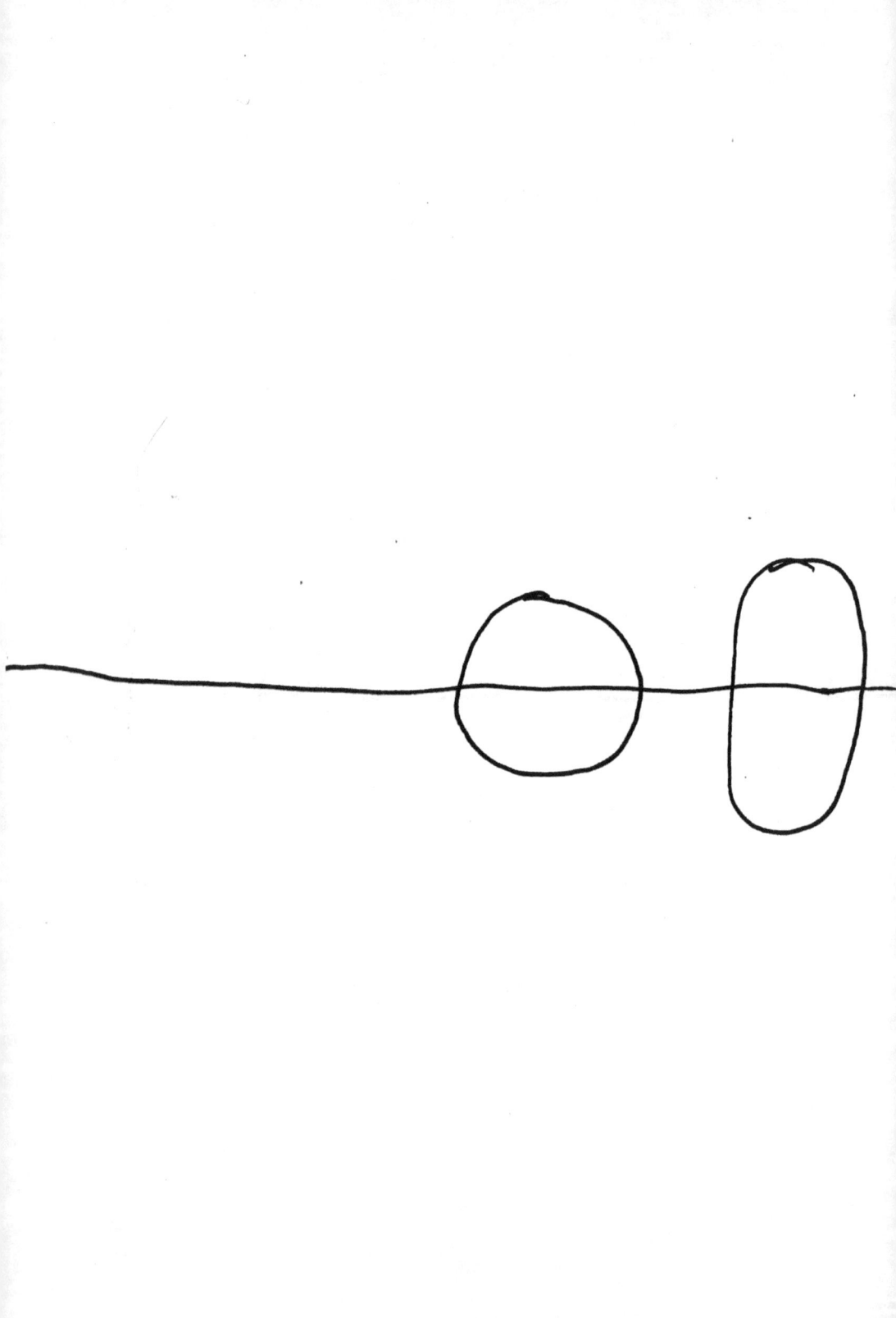

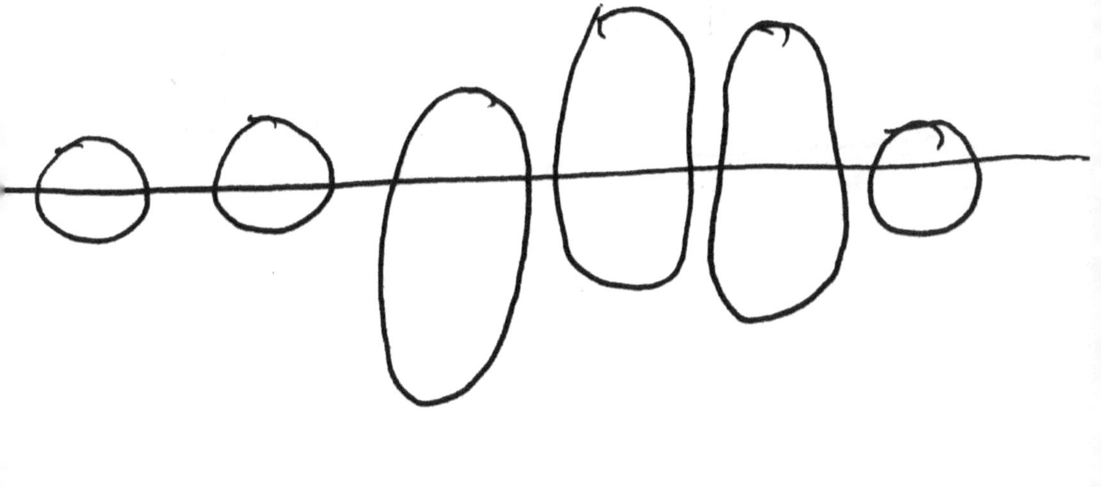

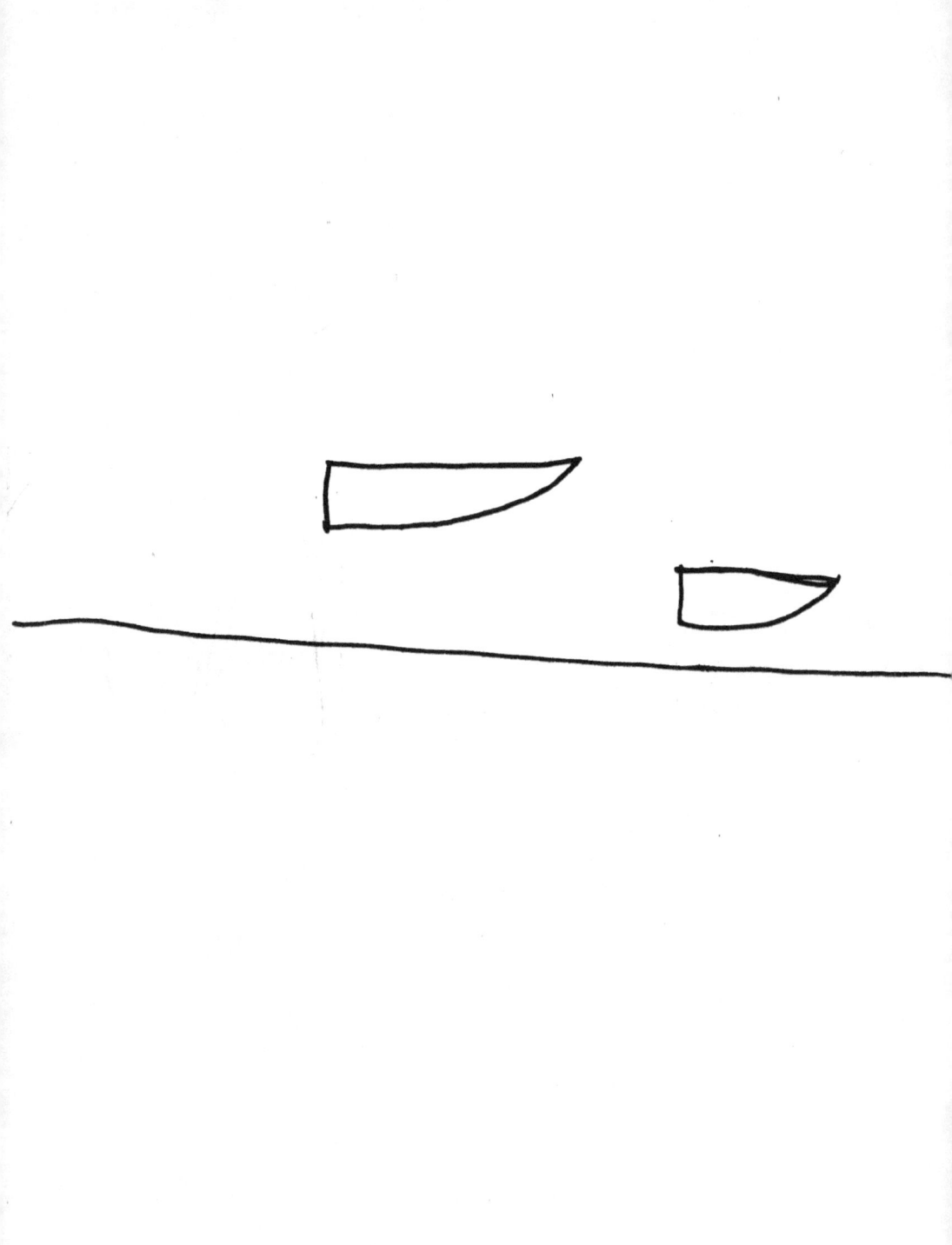

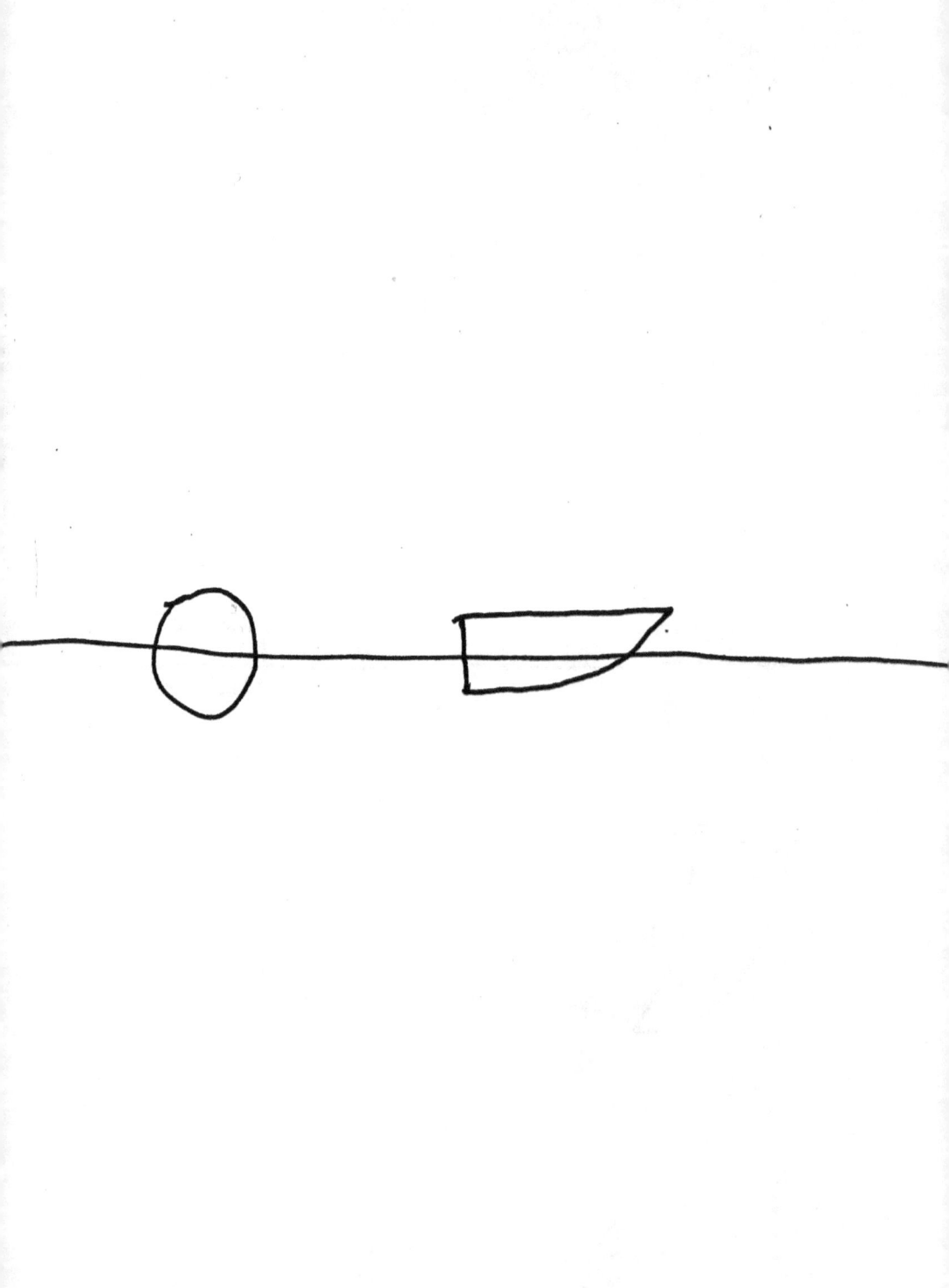

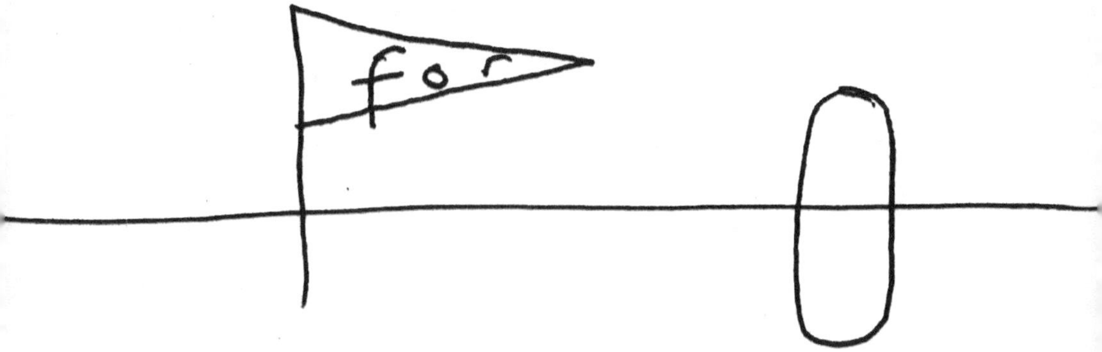
for

part
sev
en

(proof)

whisper

canned

cures

simply

fast

namet

rain

burden

seemt

pillowed

sank

form

boated

please

seem

too

to

st

oh

pleaset

painful

month

limitet

fights

flesh

stain

stone

falter

secret

air

walking

drops

mud

dragging

tooth

skies

Sing

hands

cast

same

same

s^hame

foundet

liket

forget

Cost

finger

sounds

pause

air

freshest

normal

seemt

poet

flattery

curset

eyes

really

wish

shuffle

cheek

Sound

word

Stand

word

order

easy

asking

safe

window

soart

flames

toward

fellt

crash es

number

shallow

breath

dry

bleed
ing

Something

trees

past

l ett

precious

wood

fl oor

what it was

was carrying a
sound like
spring

or like singing
reasons
like fall

or seasons making
nothing but
weight

it was hard watching
everyone's tears

knowing nothing
seemed real
enough to
be
more than
a symptom
or a
ringing ear

or maybe it was
that it became
too hard to carry
the tune
or that it was too
many times of

trying to

hold up the plate

whatever it was, the
cut was deep
enough to need a
scar

it was deep enough
to empty the
bottle

it stings enough to
watch the fall
and know I'm there
to catch It

something like the
seasons

it really seemed
like there was
enough color or sound
or singing or rain

to be a full cup ringing

and lasting

have you seen the
sun setting
over the
edge of the
distance
the trees
the
passing

it wasn't an
apology

It was a way to
say I can handle
myself

I can see that
there is enough
sky to
think about
casting
or throwing
or what if I just
need to sit a little
longer

there has to be a way
to make the
ending the
way to start

the way to find

each new

awake as

an each new

seem

as   an   each

new

way

to

begin   each   new

steeping
sound   of   the

way   pain   sounded

on   the   floor

of   the   place   to

meet   God

or   at   least   to

meet   the   way   of

slowing

if there was
a method to
understand
It
would have
been listed
already

too many ways of
hearing the
bells toll

too many times to
hear the ending
rhyme
or the

ending
like
or the
ending as just the
exact
ending with no
punctuation

It was as simple
as knowing that

there was nothing
more

there was an
ending
in the way of
starting
again

and there

is not really a
method to knowing
that the rain
sounds different
in the middle of

the
week.

passt

it was somewhere
like
knowing
that the spiral
ended
in the center

it was different
to know the
lyrics
this time
around
to know that
it was really
about being close
each time

that the bell rang

that each

time it

was really
about knowing
there was
nobody to
rely on anymore
that there
was no one to

simply name

the sound
of feeling alone

it became the feeling
of knowing that
there was
nothing at the
end of either
road

there was nothing
at the end of

each rope
or dagger
or when do you
finish singing

im still here.

I can't feel the
way to know
the touch of
sounding

as it waves the
method of feeling

the rain to
hear the names
cascading down the
cover

More like reading the
same names
to the same
reasons to
the same
cast to
the
same ending.

I'm not done.

anymore.

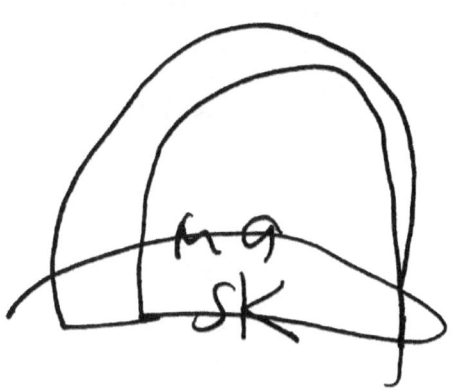

it feels like
rain falls

spring sometimes hurts
like fall

Pharm

ending

wherest

to

seem

pleg

se

t

to   th

sonded
free to
mean
the
saint

or   st

you know
free
(it comes)
with the))
chains)

if this was
the end
you wouldnt
need to
look for
more

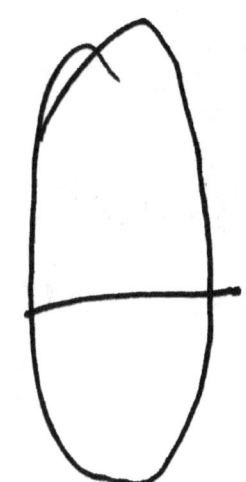

where did they
die?

when did you decide
to stop
asking?

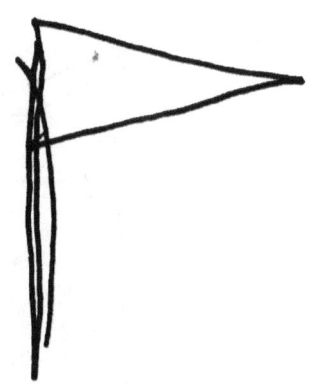

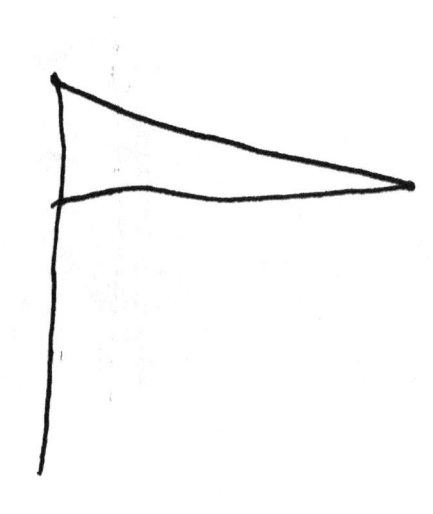

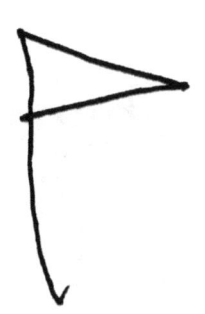

,t

Shame

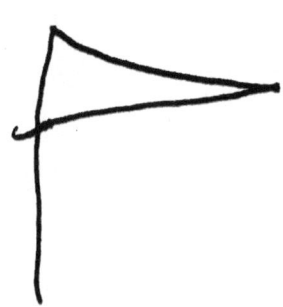